Super-Fine Valentine

by Bill Cosby
Illustrated by Varnette P. Honeywood

SCHOLASTIC INC.
New York Toronto London Auckland Sydney

Library of Congress Cataloging-in-Publication Data

Cosby, Bill, 1937-
    Super-Fine Valentine / Bill Cosby; illustrated by Varnette P. Honeywood.
      p.   cm.— (A little Bill book)
    "Cartwheel books."
    Summary: Little Bill makes a special valentine for Mia but is reluctant to give it to her, because he is afraid that the other children in their third grade class will tease him.
    ISBN 0-590-16401-5 (hardcover) 0-590-95622-1 (pbk.)
    [1. Valentine's Day— Fiction. 2. Schools— Fiction.]
  I. Honeywood, Varnette P., ill. II. Title. III. Series. IV. Series: Cosby, Bill, 1937- Little Bill book.
PZ7.C8185Su   1998
[E] — dc21   97-16563
                                                              CIP
                                                                AC

10 9 8 7 6 5 4 3 2   8 9/9 0/0 01 02

Printed in the U.S.A.   23
First printing, January 1998

To Ennis,
"Hello, friend,"
B.C.

To the Cosby Family,
Ennis's perseverance against the odds
is an inspiration to us all,
V.P.H.

Dear Parent:

A first crush can be exhilarating—and bewildering. It can make any child self-conscious and awkward, and an easy mark for teasing by other children. Even parents may joke about what seems like a cute imitation of adult behavior. But the child's feelings are tender and real.

Super-Fine Valentine portrays Little Bill's roller-coaster emotions when he discovers he likes his classmate Mia. His delight is overshadowed by his fear of being laughed at, so as he starts to tell his story, he asks the reader to PLEASE keep his secret.

Little Bill is lucky. His classmates do kid him after they catch him gazing at Mia, but only a little, and his parents refrain from teasing him when his brother betrays the reason why he's suddenly so eager to go to school.

But he still feels shy about his affection for Mia. He writes her a poem for Valentine's Day, then panics, throwing it away when she hands *him* a card. In a thoughtful move, the other boys get together and give Mia cards of their own so Little Bill can feel comfortable enough to retrieve his poem. He discovers that "it's good to tell people you like them" even if it's scary. But he really wants us to remember that it hurts to be teased when you're feeling vulnerable, so Little Bill ends his story much as he began it: "Please don't tell anyone else that I like Mia. I still don't like it when people laugh at me."

Crushes are the forerunners of mature love relationships: they deserve respect. Teasing about "being in love" can make a child believe that liking someone special is stupid, even wrong. Parents who support their child with a warm heart will teach a much better lesson.

Alvin F. Poussaint, M.D.
Clinical Professor of Psychiatry,
Harvard Medical School and
Judge Baker Children's Center,
Boston, MA

Chapter One

Hello, friend. My name is Little Bill. Can you keep a secret? This is a story about something strange that happened to me. I'll tell you about it. But, PLEASE, don't tell anyone else.

There's a girl in my class named Mia.

One day, I was watching Mia do a math worksheet when something very bad happened.

Andrew was watching me watch Mia. He pointed his finger and said, "Little Bill is in love with Mia!"

The other kids looked up from their work and said, "Ooohhh."

Our teacher, Miss Murray, heard them. She smiled. "No love stuff in the classroom," she said. "Save it for Valentine's Day tomorrow."

They all looked up from their work and giggled. That was the beginning of my troubles!

Chapter Two

On Tuesdays, I stay after school for computer club. Sometimes Mia stays for after-school art.

When computer club was over, I looked in the art room. Mia wasn't there. She wasn't at the playground, either. I started to walk home.

I walked two extra blocks so I could pass by Mia's house. Lights were on, but the curtains were closed. The door opened, and Mia's mother walked out with the family dog — a hairy dog named Max. Max had so much hair over his face, I couldn't see his eyes, nose, mouth — nothing.

"Hi, Bill," Mia's mother called to me.

"Hi, Mrs. Ford," I called back.

I put my hands in my pockets, whistled a made-up song, and walked on.

There she was! Mia and Julia
were on the swings in front of
Julia's house! And they saw me!
"Hi, Little Bill," Julia called out.
I put my head down and ran.
They giggled.

At home, I did my homework fast. Miss Murray didn't give us much to do, because she wanted us to write valentines. I picked art paper and colored pencils for Mia's valentine. I wanted to make her valentine special, so I wrote a poem.

"What rhymes with valentine?" I asked my brother Bobby.

Bobby gave me his rhyming book. It had many words that rhyme with valentine — shine, fine, mine, line, Einstein, porcupine.

"Who's Einstein?" I asked.

"He was a very smart man — a scientist," said Bobby.

Great! I thought. I was ready to write my poem.

To Mia,
You are as pretty as sunshine.
You are as smart as Einstein.
Have a super-fine Valentine's Day!

Chapter Three

The next morning, Dad knocked on my bedroom door.

"It's time to get up," he said.

"I'm up," I said.

"Start getting dressed," said Dad.

"I'm dressed," I said.

"Did you wash your face?" he asked.

"Of course!" I said. "I just took a shower!"

"But you took a shower last night," he said.

"That was ten whole hours ago," I explained.

"Then come down to breakfast."

"I already ate my breakfast. I got it myself. Cereal, milk, and juice," I said. "And I brushed my teeth! Before and after breakfast, too."

My dad was surprised that I had gotten ready all by myself. This was not the Little Bill he knew.

I went to the kitchen to get my lunch bag. Dad followed me.

"Is this really our son?" he asked my mom. "He looks like our son. But he doesn't act like our son."

"Maybe he's growing up," said Mom.

"Little Bill's in love!" said Bobby.

"I am not!" I said.

"Why don't you just tell her you like her?" Bobby asked.

"Because I'm in third grade, and in third grade you don't do that!" I said.

Bobby laughed. "That's dumb."

I put on my jacket, grabbed my backpack, and went out the door.

I walked as far as the field in front of the school. I sat behind a tree and waited until I saw Mia. Her mom kissed her good-bye and watched her cross the street.

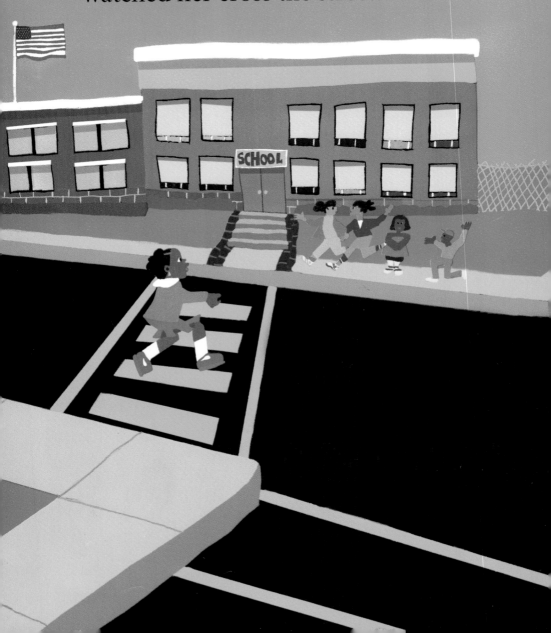

I got up from behind the tree and walked behind her. I held the valentine in my pocket. But I couldn't give it to her. My heart was scared to. I wanted to say something that would make her like me. But I didn't know what to say. I thought and thought.

Just then, Julia ran up to Mia. I moved away fast. I didn't get to say anything at all. And the valentine was still in my pocket.

After lunch, our class had a Valentine's Day party. We had heart-shaped cookies and candies and pink popcorn on red plates. We had red cranberry juice in pink cups. Then we gave each other valentines. I wanted to give Mia her card, but Michael, José, and Andrew were watching me. So I didn't. My heart was scared to.

Then I saw Mia get up from her
seat. She gave a card to Jannine, a
card to Julia, and a card to Miss
Murray. Then she walked over to
me. My heart said it was going to
burst.

Everyone giggled when Mia gave me a card. I said thank you, but I didn't give her one back. Instead, I walked over to the recycling bin and threw my card for Mia inside it.

When I walked back to my seat,
I couldn't believe what I saw.
Michael, José, and Andrew were all
giving cards to Mia!

I ran to the recycling bin, pulled
out the card, and squeezed in front
of Michael, José, and Andrew.

"Happy Valentine's Day," I said to
Mia as I handed her the card.

"We got you to give her a card," Michael said. "We knew you would do it!"

At first, I was mad. Then I smiled and thought, *It's good to show people that you like them.*

So I shared my heart-shaped
cookies and candy and my pink
popcorn with Michael, Andrew, and
José, and especially Mia.

But just the same, PLEASE don't
tell anyone else that I like Mia. I still
don't like when people laugh at me.

HOWARD L. BINGHAM

HOWARD L. BINGHAM

Bill Cosby is one of America's best-loved storytellers, known for his work as a comedian, actor, and producer. His books for adults include *Fatherhood*, *Time Flies*, *Love and Marriage*, and *Childhood*. Mr. Cosby holds a doctoral degree in education from the University of Massachusetts.

Varnette P. Honeywood, a graduate of Spelman College and the University of Southern California, is a Los Angeles-based impressive genre painter. Her work is included in many collections throughout the United States and Africa and has appeared on adult trade book jackets and in a children's book, *Let's Get the Rhythm of the Band.*

Books in the LITTLE BILL series:

The Meanest Thing to Say
All the kids are playing a new game.
You have to be mean to win it.
Can Little Bill be a winner...
and be nice, too?

The Best Way to Play
Little Bill and his friends want the
new *Space Explorers* video game.
But their parents won't buy it.
How can Little Bill and his
friends have fun without it?

The Treasure Hunt
Little Bill searches his room
for his best treasure.
What he finds is a great big surprise!

Super-Fine Valentine
Little Bill's friends are teasing him!
They say he's *in love*!
Will he get them to stop?

Shipwreck Saturday
All by himself, Little Bill built a boat out
of sticks and a piece of wood.
The older boys say that his boat won't float.
He'll show them!

Money Troubles
Funny things happen
when Little Bill tries
to earn some money.